SOCCER SNUB

BY JAKE MADDOX

Text by Elliott Smith
Illustrated by Mario Gushiken

STONE ARCH BOOKS
a capstone imprint

Published by Stone Arch Books, an imprint of Capstone
1710 Roe Crest Drive, North Mankato, Minnesota 56003
capstonepub.com

Library of Congress Cataloging-in-Publication Data
Names: Maddox, Jake, author. | Smith, Elliott, 1976– author. | Gushiken,
    Mário, illustrator.
Title: Soccer snub / Jake Maddox ; text by Elliott Smith ; illustrated by
    Mario Gushiken.
Description: North Mankato, Minnesota : Stone Arch Books, an imprint of
    Capstone, 2023. | Series: Jake Maddox sports stories | Audience: Ages
    8 to 11 | Audience: Grades 4–6 | Summary: Quincy has worked hard in
    order to move up to the A-level soccer team where he can play with his
    friend Will, but when he becomes a starter and Will is benched it seems
    like their friendship is suddenly on the rocks.
Identifiers: LCCN 2022047874 (print) | LCCN 2022047875 (ebook) |
    ISBN 9781669035084 (hardcover) | ISBN 9781669035046 (paperback) |
    ISBN 9781669035053 (pdf) | ISBN 9781669035077 (epub)
Subjects: LCSH: Soccer stories. | Teamwork (Sports)—Juvenile fiction. |
    Friendship—Juvenile fiction. | CYAC: Soccer—Fiction. | Teamwork
    (Sports)—Fiction. | Friendship—Fiction. | LCGFT: Sports fiction.
Classification: LCC PZ7.M25643 Sobn 2023 (print) | LCC PZ7.M25643
    (ebook) | DDC 813.6 [Fic]—dc23/eng/20230109
LC record available at https://lccn.loc.gov/2022047874
LC ebook record available at https://lccn.loc.gov/2022047875

Designer: Sarah Bennett

Printed and bound in China 5378

TABLE OF CONTENTS

CHAPTER ONE

TRYOUT TERROR

Quincy Green took a deep breath and opened the car door. Today was the day he'd been working toward all summer: the all-city soccer tryouts. He couldn't believe it was finally here.

"You'll do great, Quincy," his mom said from the driver's side. "Just get out there and give it everything you've got."

"That's what I'm worried about, Ma. That my best won't be enough," he said.

Quincy grabbed his water bottle and jogged toward the field. There were tons of kids running, kicking balls, and talking with each other. The soccer tryouts were a big deal for players across the city.

Quincy got about halfway to the field when a ball whizzed past his head. He jerked to a stop and looked around. He saw someone doubled over in laughter.

"That was a close one," a voice said. "I almost got you!"

Quincy was relieved to see it was his friend Will Huynh. Will was a great soccer player. He'd spent last season on the Vipers, the A-level team in the city's soccer pyramid. Quincy had been on the Copperheads, a B-level team, last season.

"Are you ready for tryouts?" Will asked while tapping another ball in the air with his foot.

"I hope so. I've been working on my skills all summer," Quincy said, taking the ball out of the air with his foot and dribbling it. "I think I'm ready to join you on the Vipers."

The boys went over to the field. When they arrived, a cluster of kids was already there, gathered around a group of coaches. Quincy didn't know most of the players from the Vipers, but he did recognize several of his teammates from the Copperheads.

"Okay, players, we're going to get started," one coach said. "Our plan is to do a series of drills and in-game scenarios to test your skills. We'll use your performance to help form our teams for the upcoming season."

Quincy did well in the sprinting and agility drills. He maneuvered the ball around the cones with ease. He teamed with Will for the passing drills and the pair connected on a variety of short and long passes. Quincy was starting to feel good about his chances.

Next up was an in-game simulation. One team would have the advantage of an extra person while they tried to score. Quincy was paired with Will, Virginia, and Norah. They were all top players on the Vipers!

The drill began at the center circle. Quincy's team would start with the ball first. He was outside in the winger's position.

The whistle blew and Quincy took off toward the goal. A moment later, the ball was passed over to Quincy. He made a quick move around a defender and looked toward the middle of the pitch. Norah streaked toward the net with her hand up, calling for a pass.

Quincy tried to deliver a perfect pass. But his foot didn't fully connect with the ball, and he sent a weak dribbler toward Norah. She slowed down to try to gain possession, but a defender came up from behind and accidentally stepped on her ankle.

"Aaaah!" Norah yelled.

TWEET! The whistle blew and several coaches sprinted out.

"She'll be okay," one of them said.

But Quincy felt terrible. Norah glared at him from the ground while holding her ankle.

Tryouts wrapped up shortly after that. Thanks to his bad pass, Quincy felt like he'd blown his shot at earning a spot on the A team.

CHAPTER TWO

THE DECISION

BLARM! BLARM! The alarm jolted Quincy awake. He felt like he hadn't slept. He'd spent most of the night reliving the tryouts, and especially the pass that led to Norah's injury. What would the coaches think?

Quincy dragged himself out of bed and went downstairs for breakfast. He wouldn't have long to wait to find out if he'd made the Vipers. The new rosters would be posted at the field at 11 a.m. He and Will had made plans to bike over and find out together. Now, he wasn't so sure if that was a good idea.

Quincy didn't have much time to linger in his thoughts. A *TAP-TAP-TAP* sound came from the front door.

Quincy ran to the door and flung it open. Will stood outside on the front step with his bike parked behind him.

"You ready to find out the teams?" he said with a smile.

"Not really," Quincy replied. "But I guess I have no choice."

Quincy grabbed his helmet and bike out of the garage. Then the boys pedaled through town to the soccer fields. During the brief ride, Quincy's nerves disappeared. But as soon as he pulled up to the fields and saw a group of kids gathered, Quincy's stomach flip-flopped like he was riding a roller coaster.

Will jumped off his bike and practically sprinted toward the list of names. "Here we go!" he shouted.

Quincy approached the board slowly. This was the moment of truth. He pushed past a couple of kids and scanned the list. The one for the Vipers read . . .

Aaron Franklin

Sharon Gould

Quincy Green

Will Huynh

Quincy didn't even look at the rest of the names on the list. He'd made it!

Quincy pumped his fist in celebration. He turned to find Will coming toward him with a big smile on his face.

"You made it, man!" Will said. "I can't wait to be teammates."

Several of Quincy's old teammates from the Copperheads came over to congratulate him. Quincy was the only person to move up to the Vipers this season.

"Let's meet the rest of the team," Will said, pushing Quincy toward a group of kids standing nearby.

"Hey guys, this is my friend Quincy," Will said. "He's the newest member of the Vipers. He's going to help us get to the championship this year."

A couple of kids stepped up to give Quincy high fives.

"Good to have you on the team," one girl said. "My name is Sharon."

Suddenly, there was a commotion near the group. A couple of team members stepped aside as Norah limped toward them.

"Hmm, seems like he's only good enough to get people hurt," Norah said with a sneer.

"Yeah, I'm really sorry about . . ." Quincy started to say. But Norah turned her back to him. Then she and a big group of teammates walked away.

"Ah, don't worry about them," Will said. "Once we start playing, she'll forget all about that."

"I'm sure you're right," Quincy said, but he didn't believe it. The Vipers were a close-knit team. And Quincy was definitely the new guy. While he was still excited about making the squad, the team's frosty welcome made him feel like he had a lot of work to do to make some new friends.

"C'mon, let's go back to your house and kick the ball around," Will said.

Quincy nodded and headed back toward their bikes. He couldn't wait for practice to prove to Norah and the rest of the Vipers that he was a good teammate.

CHAPTER THREE

COLD FEET

A few days later, Quincy arrived at the field for the Vipers' first practice of the season. He was determined to make a good impression.

Quincy found Will and gave him a fist bump. He made eye contact with Norah, but she frowned and turned to whisper to the person next to her. They started laughing. Quincy sighed. He assumed they were talking about him.

TWEET!! A sharp whistle jolted everyone to attention. A woman jogged out in front of the team.

"Hello, Vipers!" she said. "I'm Coach Ally. As you may know, Coach Dan retired after last season, so I'm your new coach. I'm really excited to get to know you all and help you play better soccer."

Quincy was pleased. *A new coach means no more old ways,* he thought.

"My strategy is based on speed," Coach Ally continued. "I think we have the talent to outrun and tire out anyone we play. We're going to be a fast-paced, attacking team."

Quincy saw some heads turn and a couple of mumbles. But this strategy seemed good to him.

I almost always win when we race in gym class, he thought with a thrill.

Will leaned over and whispered, "She seems cool."

Quincy nodded. "Yeah, I think she's going to be a fun coach to play for."

Coach Ally opened a large bag of balls. "Okay, team, let's get started. I want to get an idea of how you will perform in high-pressure situations. We'll practice trying to score a goal in the last five minutes of the match."

The team ran onto the pitch. Quincy was ready to show Coach what he could do. He took a spot on the wing and when Coach blew the whistle, his side started with the ball. Quincy ran toward the goal, speeding past his defender. He was wide open, with a good look at the goal. But Norah passed the ball to the other side of the field, where it was stolen by the defense.

Quincy continued to feel snubbed by the rest of the team all the way through practice. He worked hard to get free but no one but Will would pass him the ball. Quincy grew more frustrated as practice went along.

"Hey, I'm open! Pass me the ball," he shouted to Darin.

"Oops, I didn't see you," Darin said.

With just minutes until the end of practice, Will lofted a ball down the left side. Quincy turned on the jets and raced past his defender to corral the ball. This was his chance! He gathered the ball with his foot and . . . shot it way over the goal into the brush behind the net.

"Way to go get that ball, Quincy!" Coach Ally shouted.

But Quincy felt discouraged as practice came to an end. The rest of the Vipers were buzzing about, but Quincy felt like he hadn't done anything.

"Quincy, wasn't that practice fun?" Will said. "You almost had a great goal!"

Quincy didn't feel like explaining what was bothering him. Will wouldn't understand. He didn't want to dim his friend's excitement. So he said, "That was a really nice pass."

As he walked to his mom's car, Quincy wrestled with a dilemma. How could he show the Vipers what he could do if his teammates never passed him the ball?

CHAPTER FOUR

ON THE OUTS

Three days later, Quincy was fired up for the next practice. He was set on having a positive attitude. He remembered a saying that his mother taught him: *You catch more flies with honey.* In this case, it meant being nice to the people who were mean, hoping they'll change their opinion.

So Quincy packed a small cooler filled with MegaJuice, the energy drink that everyone liked. He planned on passing it out after practice and getting to know the rest of the team. But he knew who he had to start with for his plan to work.

When he arrived at the field, Quincy scanned the area. He spotted Norah on the sidelines, tying up her cleats, and he made a beeline straight toward her.

"Hey, Norah, how are you doing today?" Quincy asked.

"Hmph," Norah grunted without looking up from her laces.

"Anyway . . . I just wanted to say I'm really happy to be on the Vipers with you and the rest of the team," Quincy said, plowing forward. "I know we're going to do well once the games get started."

Norah looked up from her shoes but didn't say anything. Quincy's nerve faltered.

"Uh, umm, who's your favorite soccer team?" Quincy stammered.

By this time, a few other players had gathered around. Quincy gave a weak smile to welcome them as Norah stood up.

"Look, Quincy, the Vipers were doing just fine without you," she said. "We made it to the regional semifinals last year. You can't just come in here and think you're going to take over our team."

"But I don't want—" Quincy started.

"You're messing up our chemistry," Norah continued. "So why don't you just get used to sitting on the bench and let the rest of us play."

"Hey," a voice shouted behind him. Quincy turned and was relieved to see Will approaching. "You guys need to give Quincy a chance. He's a great player. We've been working together all summer. He can help get us to the top."

"Will, you're just saying that because he's your friend," Norah said, and the rest of the Vipers nodded in agreement. With that, Norah and the others walked away.

Quincy's shoulders sagged. His plan had gone *poof* before practice had even started.

"Thanks for sticking up for me, Will," Quincy said.

"Norah doesn't remember when she was the new kid on the team," Will said. "Don't let her bring you down."

It was too late for that. Quincy wasn't even sure he wanted to play for the Vipers anymore. Maybe he could go back to the B team and have fun with his old teammates.

Quincy went through practice in a daze. When it was over, he didn't even bother handing out the MegaJuice. He grabbed his cooler and trudged back to the car, where his mom was waiting.

"Did your teammates like the beverages?" she asked.

"Oh, someone else had already brought some," he lied.

Quincy thought about his options all the way home from practice. By the time they pulled into the garage, he had made up his mind.

He was going to quit the Vipers. Playing with them just wasn't very fun.

CHAPTER FIVE

SPEED RULES

The next day, Quincy was watching the London FC soccer match on TV in the basement when he heard a knock at the door.

"Quincy, it's for you!" his dad shouted.

Quincy heard some clomping footsteps above. Then Will came bounding down the stairs.

"Hey, you want to practice for a while?" Will asked. "We've got the first game coming up soon."

"Sure," Quincy said. He grabbed his ball and followed Will back up the stairs.

The boys went to the backyard to kick the ball around. Quincy lightly bounced the ball off his head, trying to think of the best way to share his decision with Will.

"So, about that first game," Quincy finally said. "I'm not sure I'm going to stay on the Vipers. I don't think I'm ready to play with you guys. One more season on the Copperheads will be good for me."

Will kicked his own ball and knocked Quincy's out of the air, causing Quincy to flinch.

"That's crazy!" Will said, picking up his ball. "You're an awesome soccer player. I think your real issue is Norah and those jerks on the team. I told you not to let them get in your head!"

"But they have," Quincy said. "I want to play *and* have fun, and I haven't been having fun on the Vipers."

Will kicked the ball back to Quincy.
"I get it," he said quietly. "But just play the first game before you make a final decision."

I really do want to wear the Vipers' red jersey, Quincy thought.

"Okay, I'll give it one game before I decide for sure," he said.

"Yes!" Will shouted. "Now let's get ready to beat the Bees!"

* * *

A few days later, Quincy arrived at the field for the Vipers' first game. He was both excited and nervous at the same time. He stood next to Will as Coach Ally delivered her final set of instructions.

"Remember, team, the name of the game is speed," Coach Ally said, pointing at a diagram on her clipboard. "We want to use it to get past the Bees' defenders and take good shots on goal. One, two, three, Vipers!"

Quincy started the game by sitting on the bench. He cheered on his teammates when they gained possession of the ball and when Alberto made a save in goal. Most importantly, he stayed ready to get in the game at a moment's notice.

His moment came in the second half, in the 60th minute of the 90-minute game. The score was tied 1–1.

"Quincy!" Coach Ally shouted. "You're in for Aaron."

Quincy leaped off the bench and stood next to the official. The official waved him onto the pitch as Aaron ran off.

Quincy took his position as winger and began running alongside his defender. Almost immediately, Quincy had a realization.

I'm faster than he is, he thought. As the minutes ticked away, the Vipers looked for an opportunity to break the tie.

With about a minute left, a bad Bees pass led to a breakaway for the Vipers. Quincy surged past his defender and, surprisingly, Sharon passed him the ball. He was running right for the goal! He looked to his left and saw Will streaking down the right side.

Quincy booted a pass along the mouth of the goal and . . . Will stuck his foot out to deflect it into the corner of the net!

GOAL! The Vipers grabbed a 2–1 lead!

Two minutes later, the referee blew the whistle, signaling the end of the game.

The Vipers celebrated on their bench. Will and Quincy exchanged high fives. For the first time, Quincy felt like he was part of the team.

CHAPTER SIX

DEFROSTING

The Vipers' next game was scheduled for a week later against the Monarchs. To get ready, Quincy and Will did some scouting at the Monarchs' matchup against the Mantises.

The Monarchs played a zone defense that made it difficult for their opponents to find scoring opportunities. Instead of a traditional one-on-one defense where each defender stayed with one person, a zone defense relied on space. Defenders stayed within a certain zone, and once a player went beyond them, the responsibility was passed to the teammate behind them.

The boys talked about strategies the Vipers could use to beat the zone defense. Will suggested switching attackers from side to side. Quincy thought the Vipers could make diagonal runs toward the goal to confuse the defense. Either way, it would be a tough challenge.

When game day arrived, Quincy thought he might be part of the starting lineup. However, he was disappointed to find himself sitting on the bench again.

This game unfolded very differently than the previous one. The Monarchs did a good job neutralizing the Vipers' speed. By halftime, the score was still 0–0.

"Good job out there, team," Coach Ally said. "We have to stick to our game plan. Eventually they will get tired, and then we can break through their defense." She paused and scanned the bench. "Quincy, you're in for the second half."

Will fist-bumped Quincy. "Let's try to make something happen," he whispered.

On the field, Quincy experienced the Monarchs' excellent defense for himself. He felt like two defenders were always in his path. The Monarchs played like they were happy with a scoreless tie. But Quincy wasn't.

The next time he got the ball, he dribbled hard toward the goal. Two defenders closed in, ready to steal the ball.

Quincy figured that would happen, so he used a backheel pass to flick the ball to Norah, who was a few steps behind him. She fired the ball past the surprised goalie to give the Vipers a 1–0 lead!

"Great pass," she said, giving Quincy a high five.

After the Vipers took the lead, the Monarchs seemed deflated. Their defense was not as sharp as it was before.

Late in the game, Will used some fancy footwork to dribble around a Monarchs defender. He fired a low, fast pass, and Quincy quickly booted the ball toward the top right corner of the goal. It zipped past the leaping goalie and into the back of the net. Quincy had scored his first goal with the Vipers!

Quincy and Will did a jumping chest bump to celebrate the goal.

"That was awesome!" Quincy exclaimed.

Five minutes later, it was all over. The Monarchs never threatened to score and the Vipers wrapped up their second straight win. As Quincy gathered his things on the sideline, he noticed someone walking up to him.

"Great game, Quincy," Norah said. Quincy looked shocked, while Norah looked somewhat embarrassed. "Um, sorry about giving you a hard time before. I guess I wasn't being very nice. We're happy to have you on the team."

Several other Vipers players came over to clap Quincy on the back and give him fist bumps. Quincy could barely contain his smile.

Will walked over with a knowing look on his face. "What did I tell you?" he said. "Once they saw you play, they'd be all in."

"You were right," Quincy admitted. "I'm glad I listened to you and stuck with it."

As Quincy and Will walked toward the parking lot, Norah stopped them. "Hey, do you guys want to go to The Creamery with us to get some ice cream?"

"Sure!" Quincy said. He and Will joined the group. Quincy felt like things were finally looking up.

CHAPTER SEVEN

LINEUP DRAMA

The next day, Quincy sprinted out of his parents' car as soon as they arrived at the field for practice. He was ready to learn more and keep the Vipers' winning streak alive. A group of teammates waved him over to talk.

"Hey, Quincy," Norah said. "Practice should be fun today. Coach says we're going to put in a new game plan."

"Really?" Quincy said. "But we've been doing so well."

When Will arrived, he immediately started working on his ball-handling skills. He dribbled quickly and bounced the ball between his feet.

"Why do you think Coach is changing things up?" Quincy wondered.

"It's because our next game is against the Grasshoppers," Will said. "They're always one of the toughest teams in the league."

The whistle blew to signal the start of practice. Now that he truly felt like part of the team, Quincy had a great practice. His passes were sharp, he scored a couple of goals, and he ran faster than ever.

His connection with Will was still strong, but now, Quincy and Norah started working well together. Quincy was fast enough to track down Norah's long outlet passes, and Norah was awesome at handling Quincy's crosses into the box.

I've got to be in the starting lineup now,
Quincy thought.

When practice ended, Coach Ally asked the team to stick around for a minute. "So far, we've been playing great soccer," she said. "But I do want to make some changes to the lineup so that we can maximize our potential. I like to be up-front about our lineup changes so there are no surprises."

Quincy looked over at Will, who winked.

"The biggest move is to our starters," she continued. "Quincy, you're going to move into the starting eleven so we can take advantage of your speed. Will, we're going to have you coming off the bench moving forward. I want to use your ball skills late in the game as our opponents get tired."

Oh no, Quincy thought. *Will just got benched!* He snuck a quick glance over at Will, who was bright red with anger.

Coach spoke for a few more minutes and then let the group go. Quincy quickly went over to his friend, who was yanking off his cleats.

"Will, I'm sorry—"

"Don't worry about it," Will said gruffly. "Congrats on taking my spot."

"I didn't mean—" Quincy started, but Will stood up to leave.

"Hey, do you want to hang out at my house today?" Quincy asked.

"No," Will said.

"What about tomorrow? We could watch the match on TV," Quincy offered.

"No!" Will yelled and ran toward the parking lot.

Quincy thought about his friend the whole ride home. He knew what it felt like to get snubbed, and now Will was experiencing the same thing.

Quincy wanted to let Will know things would work out. When he got home, he sent a quick text: *Sorry about today. Let's work together to get you back in the starting lineup.*

He checked his phone every few minutes before he went to bed. But Will didn't respond.

Quincy was bummed. He'd gotten what he wanted, but it seemed like he lost a friend in the process.

CHAPTER EIGHT

JOINING FORCES

Quincy tossed and turned all night. He was worried about his friendship with Will. He didn't want soccer to come between them, especially since they both loved playing the sport.

The next morning, Will still hadn't replied to Quincy's text. And he was pretty sure going over to Will's house wouldn't be a good idea. How would his friend act during the Vipers' next practice?

I need to figure out a plan, Quincy thought.

While eating his breakfast, Quincy sat up with a jolt. He had an idea, but it would involve taking a chance on someone new.

After wolfing down his toast, Quincy hopped on his bike and rode a few streets over. He approached the door slowly and knocked.

"Quincy? What are you doing here?" Norah said as she opened the door with a surprised look on her face.

"Well, I think Will is pretty mad about losing his starting spot," Quincy said. "He won't talk to me, so I'm hoping maybe you could help."

"Hmm, I can try," Norah said. Then she pointed at Quincy's T-shirt. "Do you like London FC? From the English League?"

"Yeah, they're my all-time favorite team!" Quincy said.

"Mine too!" Norah said. "I'm about to watch their game. Do you want to come in and join me?"

Quincy settled into Norah's couch to watch the first half. The new friends cheered on their favorite team and marveled at the skill of the top players in the world.

At halftime, their conversation turned to the Vipers and their upcoming game.

"You know how London FC plays with a unique formation?" Norah said, rubbing her chin. "What if our team did something like that? If we did, we could use Will's excellent ball-handling skills."

Quincy thought about it for a second. "Show me what you're thinking," he replied.

Norah grabbed a piece of paper and scribbled Xs on a hand-drawn soccer field.

"I think we should try playing a three-three-four formation," Norah said.

Quincy looked at the diagram and all the Xs on the field. The formation had three defenders, three midfielders, and four attackers. It would certainly catch the Grasshoppers by surprise. But it was also a risky formation.

"This could get Will back on the field since we have an extra attacker," Quincy said. "But it would be tough on our defense."

"I know," Norah said. "But we haven't been able to beat the Grasshoppers in two years. We lost to them in the regular season and in the playoffs last year. So, maybe we should try something different."

"Should we call Will and tell him about this?" Quincy wondered. He was eager to give his friend some good news.

"Well, we're going to have to check with Coach Ally first," Norah said. "I don't know if she'll go for it."

As the second half of the London FC game unfolded, Quincy wondered if the plan they'd come up with would work. London FC was winning the game at halftime, but they made some defensive errors in the second half.

Quincy and Norah's favorite team lost its match playing an unusual formation. Would the same thing happen to the Vipers?

CHAPTER NINE

GET IN FORMATION

Two days later, Quincy and Norah got to practice a few minutes early. When they arrived, they saw Coach Ally setting up cones and nets.

"Hey guys, what's going on?" Coach said.

"Well . . ." Quincy started, only to hesitate. He was the new kid on the team—should he really be asking the coach to make changes?

"We were hoping we could talk with you about a new formation for the Grasshoppers game," Norah said, showing her the diagram.

"This way, we can use our team speed and Will's ball-handling skills from the start," Quincy added.

Coach Ally studied the diagram. She scrunched her face and then started drawing her own imaginary lines on the paper with the tip of her finger.

"Did you guys come up with this on your own?" Coach Ally asked.

"Yes, we did," Quincy said with a grin. "We were inspired while watching London FC, our favorite team."

Coach Ally nodded knowingly. "I'm open to trying this. I like that you're thinking about the game and how to get better," she said. "It's always good to listen to new voices, even as a coach."

Quincy glanced at Norah with a look of surprise. Then he turned back to Coach Ally and said, "I think it will work."

"We might give up goals if we don't execute this formation perfectly," she continued. "But it's worth a shot."

Quincy and Norah smiled. They had done it! They could see the rest of the team trickling in for practice. They zeroed in on Will, who was trudging toward the field.

"Will, we've got some really great news," Quincy said.

"Wait," Will replied. "I want to apologize. I shouldn't have gotten upset about the lineup. I'm happy for you. And I know I can still make a difference coming off the bench."

The two friends shook hands. Quincy was relieved that things were getting back to normal.

"Yeah, about the bench," Norah said. Quincy and Norah explained to Will about the new 3-3-4 formation and how it meant Will would return to the starting lineup.

"Wow," Will said. "That's awesome! But will it work?"

"I don't know," Quincy said. "But we've got one practice to learn it."

They ran over to join the rest of the team. Coach Ally pulled out her large whiteboard and sketched Quincy and Norah's formation on it. She began explaining how it would work to the team. She told the Vipers about the positives and the negatives of the setup.

"The Grasshoppers were a tough team last season," Aaron said. "Will this give us a better shot at beating them?"

"I think it will help," Coach Ally said to cheers from the team.

Practice was hard. Trying to learn a new formation was more difficult than anyone expected. There were some major mistakes at first. Players ran to the wrong positions. Defensive errors led to easy goals.

Slowly, though, the Vipers began to figure things out. Four attackers gave the team plenty of chances to score goals. The team was exhausted when Coach Ally blew the whistle to end practice.

Quincy felt optimistic. "I think this idea is going to work," he said to his friends.

But if it didn't, would the team blame him?

CHAPTER TEN

TRIPLE THREAT

Quincy woke up early on game day. He had crafted a whole routine in advance of the big afternoon showdown with the Grasshoppers. It started with studying London FC games. Then he kicked the ball against the side of his house for the rest of the morning.

By the time he got to the field, Quincy was ready for action. But he was caught off-guard by the number of fans who were already there. The stands were packed!

The Vipers were nervous. This was their toughest opponent of the season. Coach Ally gathered the team before kickoff.

"Remember, speed is the key," she said. "This new formation will help us get good looks at the goal. Keep shooting!"

The Vipers ran out to the field. Quincy took his position on the right wing. Norah was on the left wing, and Will and Sharon were in the middle of the four-person alignment along the center circle.

The Grasshoppers looked surprised at the formation. They whispered and pointed. Quincy thought they were trying to figure out which player they would defend.

TWEET! The whistle blew to start the game. The Grasshoppers attacked right away. The Vipers were caught flat-footed. The Grasshoppers' top player whizzed past Quincy and the rest of the Vipers' defense crumbled.

The Grasshoppers' star dribbled down the field and fired a rising shot from just outside the box. Alberto jumped to tip the ball away, but it soared over his fingers and into the net.

Just like that, the score was 1–0 in favor of the Grasshoppers!

After the goal, the Vipers seemed out of sync. They played tentatively, scared to make another mistake.

For the rest of the half, Quincy never had a good opportunity with the ball, and the Grasshoppers took control. By halftime, the Vipers sagged onto the bench, still trailing 1–0.

"Team, we are still in this game," Coach Ally said. "You guys wanted to use this formation, but we haven't *done* anything with it. Let's be more aggressive in the second half."

Even though he was new, Quincy decided now was a good time to speak up.

"There's plenty of room in the middle of the field," he said. "Will, you can get in there with your footwork. Then look for me and Norah on the wings. You can send long passes in. We can get them."

Will nodded and Norah smiled. The plan was set.

Ten minutes into the second half, the opportunity arose. Will got the ball around midfield. He did a quick deke around one defender and spotted Norah running down the left side.

Will flicked a pass in her direction. Norah controlled the ball and blasted a low rocket past the diving goalie. The game was tied!

The match stayed that way for a while. But in the 88th minute, Quincy forced a turnover. He took the ball off the foot of a Grasshoppers player and made a quick pass to Will.

Will zipped toward the goal. Once again, he found Norah wide and booted the ball as two Grasshoppers came over to steal.

Norah chipped the high pass toward the net. Then Quincy leaped high in the air and headed the ball past the goalie!

The Vipers took a 2–1 lead!

Less than two minutes later, the game was over. The Vipers all celebrated at midfield.

"We did it! We beat the Grasshoppers thanks to you, Quincy!" Norah yelled.

"Oh man, I'm so glad you stayed on the team!" Will said.

Quincy smiled in the chaos and hugged his friends. "It was a team effort," he said. "Old and new can come together to create something great."

The new friends walked off the field to the sounds of cheers.

AUTHOR BIO

photo by Elliott Smith

Elliott Smith has written more than 40 chapter books for young readers in a variety of topics. He previously worked as a sports reporter for newspapers. He lives in Falls Church, Virginia, with his wife and two children. He loves reading, watching sports, going to concerts, and adding to his collection of Pittsburgh Steelers memorabilia.

ILLUSTRATOR BIO

photo by Mario Gushiken

Mario Gushiken is a digital artist from São Paulo, Brazil. Drawing was a hobby for him as a child, and he is very happy to have turned it into his career. Inspired by cartoons and video games, Mario began working as a graphic designer and illustrator in 2014. In 2020, he became a full-time freelance illustrator. In his spare time, Mario likes to hang out with friends and play video games.

GLOSSARY

aggressive (uh-GREH-siv)—strong and forceful

agility (uh-GI-luh-tee)—relating to the ability to move fast and easily

chemistry (KE-mis-tree)—the emotional and psychological interaction between people

deke (DEEK)—to pretend to go one way, then go in the other direction; it is a move used to trick opposing players

formation (for-MAY-shuhn)—the way in which members of a team are arranged

maneuver (muh-NOO-ver)—to make planned and controlled movements that require practiced skills

neutralize (NOO-truh-lize)—to stop something from working or having an effect

roster (ROSS-tur)—a list of players on a team

scout (SKOWT)—to watch another team to learn about the way they play

simulation (sim-yuh-LAY-shuhn)—a practice run to imitate a situation

strategy (STRAT-uh-jee)—a plan for winning a game

DISCUSSION QUESTIONS

1. Why do you think Norah and the rest of the Vipers were mean to Quincy at the start of the season?

2. Why did Coach Ally go along with Quincy and Norah's idea to play with a 3-3-4 formation? Would you have made the same decision? Why or why not?

3. What do you think Quincy should do to make a new player feel welcome on the Vipers next season?

WRITING PROMPTS

1. Think about a time when you were a new person at school or on a team. How did you feel? Write a paragraph that explains your experience and offers advice to someone who is going through the same thing.

2. How would you feel if one of your friends suddenly took your starting spot on a team? Pretend you're Will and write a response to Quincy's text.

3. Have you ever been scared to speak up and suggest doing something a different way? Write about a time you overcame your fears and did something that was uncomfortable.

MORE ABOUT
SOCCER FORMATIONS

Formations refer to the positions of the players on the pitch, not including the goalkeeper.

The type, or nature, of a formation depends on how aggressive or defensive a team wants to be during a game.

Teams may change their formation from game to game to try to fool the opponent. Some teams always stay with the same formation, no matter who they play.

- The most common soccer formation is the 4-4-2. That means there are four defenders, four midfielders, and two attackers.

- The 4-3-3 formation moves an additional player into an attacking position. A team may switch to this formation if they are losing and want to try to score a quick goal.

- A 4-5-1 is a defensive formation. With five midfielders clogging the middle of the pitch, it is a great way to possess the ball and run the clock down.

- The 4-3-2-1 is known as the Christmas tree formation. Imagine four defenders at the back, three midfielders, two attackers, and one striker. The shape on the pitch looks like a Christmas tree!

- The 3-3-4 formation that the Vipers switch to against the Grasshoppers is very rare in modern soccer. However, it was a popular formation in the 1950s and 1960s. Occasionally, teams use it to catch their opponents off-guard.

While most teams will start in a specific formation, they can change formations during a game if needed. If a team is losing in the final minutes of an important game, their goalkeeper might come out of the box to help on the offensive attack!